Contents

Published by
Trinity College London
E music@trinitycollege.com
www.trinitycollege.com

Cover and book design by as creatives
Brand development by Alistair Crane
Audio produced and mixed by Ross Power (RP Music), Terl Bryant and Matt Hay
Tracks arranged by composers and Mike Simpson, Alice Hall, Nick Powlesland

Registered in the UK
Company no. 02683033
Charity no. 1014792

What is Music Tracks?

Music Tracks is a programme for young musicians who learn in whole-class and small-group environments. It aims to inspire them, right from when they first pick up an instrument, to explore the work of musicians and composers from the world around them. It promotes creative and collaborative music-making through exciting repertoire and resources, setting young learners on the road to becoming lifelong music-makers.

Music Tracks is made up of two strands:

First Access Track is a package of materials supporting whole-class instrumental and vocal teaching. It includes a wide range of original music, backing tracks and resources.

Small Group Tracks are exams and resources for small-group learning. They are designed to follow on from First Access Track, but are equally suitable for learners who did not begin their learning through First Access Track.

This book supports Small Group Tracks at Initial level. It contains everything needed to prepare for and take an Initial Small Group Track exam, and has been designed as a useful resource for small-group teaching.

Find out more about Music Tracks at www.trinitycollege.com/musictracks

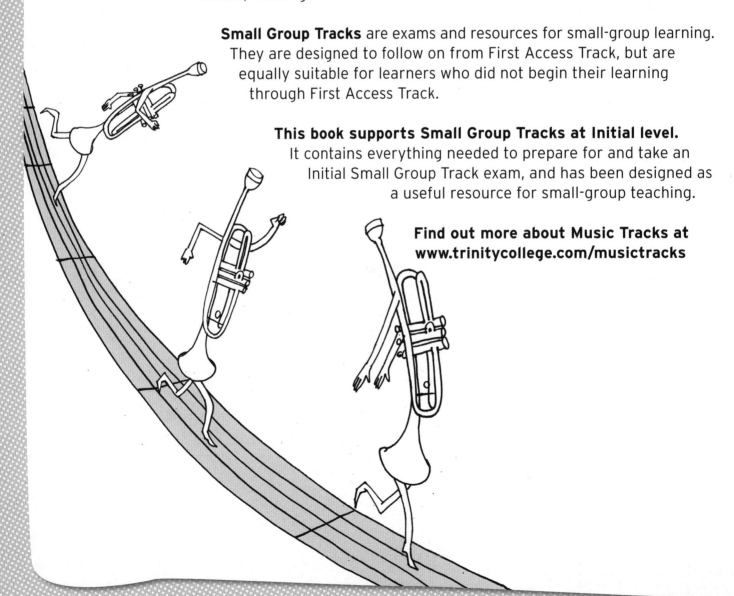

What are Small Group Tracks?

Small Group Tracks are exams and resources for small-group learning. The exams are taken by groups of two to four learners, each of whom is featured as a solo performer in every section of the exam. The learners are assessed by a specially trained Music Tracks examiner, and each receives their own certificate and report form. Supporting resources are provided in a series of Small Group Tracks books, designed to integrate with small-group learning strategies in order to promote holistic musical development.

The exam

Exams are offered at three different levels: Initial, Track 1 and Track 2 (equivalent to Initial, Grade 1 and Grade 2), supporting carefully graded musical progression. In the exam, the group plays three pieces from the relevant Small Group Tracks book, including one Technical Piece. The group also performs one Musicianship Skills test, either Copyback or Improvising. Each learner is assessed as an individual, receiving comments and marks relating to their own performance.

The music

The music draws on styles and genres from around the world and from different periods. Most of the pieces are original compositions, and many include lyrics to encourage aural development through singing or speaking. The pieces in Group A include ensemble and solo sections, allowing learners to demonstrate both types of playing. The pieces in Group B – the Technical Pieces – require learners to take it in turns to play phrases, showing that they understand shape and structure. These pieces also focus on specific technical elements.

The resources

As well as containing everything needed to prepare for the exam, each Small Group Tracks book is packed with ideas and material for small-group teaching, supporting a varied curriculum of learning. Each piece is accompanied by a high-quality backing track, and there is background information on the style of each piece, as well as hints and tips for preparation. Additional resources for teachers and learners are available online – visit www.trinitycollege.com/musictracks for details of how to access these.

The exam at a glance

In the exam, the group performs the following items in the order below:

Piece 1 - a piece from Group A in this book

Piece 2 - a different piece from Group A in this book

Piece 3 - a Technical Piece from Group B in this book

Musicianship Skills - either Copyback or Improvising

Please note that all learners in the group must present the same pieces and Musicianship Skills test. Note also that the repeated section in the Group A pieces must be played as many times as there are learners in the group, so that each learner gets the chance to perform this section as a soloist. All pieces and Musicianship Skills tests are played with a backing track.

Note for teachers

All the pieces in this book have been edited with regard to current performance practice. Dynamics and articulation should be observed except where otherwise stated.

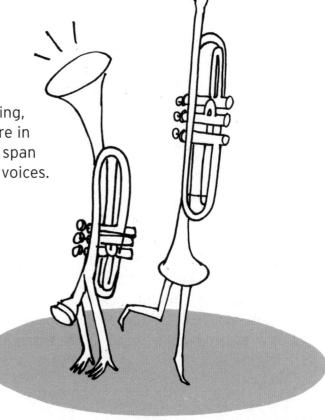

Lyrics have been provided as a tool for aural learning, either through singing or speaking. Please take care in the use of lyrics for singing, as some of the pieces span ranges that may not be appropriate for all singing voices. Lyrics should not be used in the exam.

If you are preparing for an exam, please check www.trinitycollege.com/musictracks for the most up-to-date version of the syllabus, as this may change from time to time.

Group A
Township Time

During the apartheid era in South Africa, urban 'townships' were established by the government as residential areas for native Africans. Under this racial segregation, various styles of music developed, influenced by the hymns taught in missionary schools, and by the jazz which Americans brought to the country during the gold rush. **Township Time** has a simple chord structure, with added jazzy harmonies and a syncopated bass line, combining to give the up-tempo, bouncy feel that is typical of the township style.

When you play this piece make the first section *legato*, with a 'laid-back' feel, and then make the *staccato* notes at bar 17 really punchy, for contrast. You should play the repeated section as many times as there are learners in your group, so that everyone gets a chance to perform the solo section.

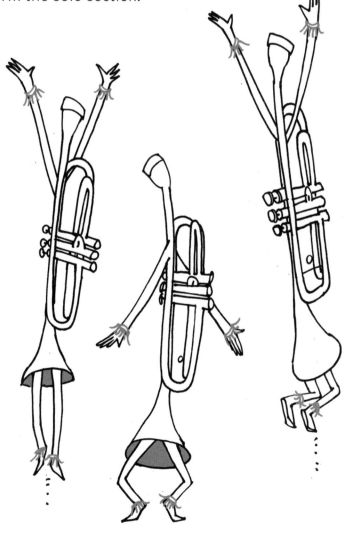

Township Time

♩ = 105

P Christmas

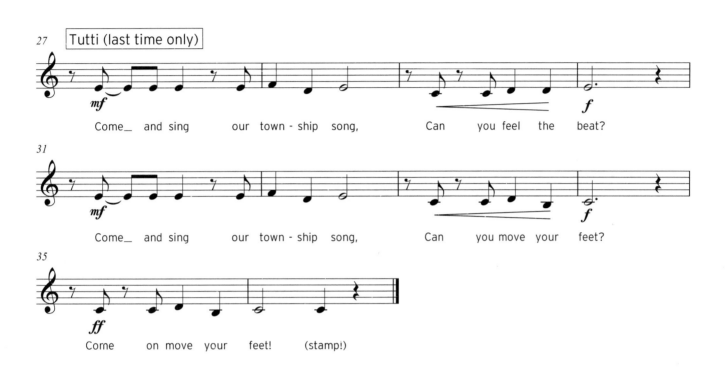

Group A
Bhangra Beat

Bhangra is a British Asian phenomenon, a fusion of Punjabi folk music, Western pop music and Bollywood film music. With immigration to the UK from the Punjab in the 1970s, Bhangra music became increasingly popular, and many groups were formed to perform at weddings and cultural festivals. Live groups use standard rock/pop instruments such as electric guitar and bass, keyboards and drum kit, as well as *dhol*, *dholak* and *tabla*, which are all Indian drums.

When you play this piece, don't swing the melody too much – a gentle 'lilt' is more stylistic. Emphasise the accented notes at the beginning and ends of the phrases to add punch to your playing. You should play the repeated section as many times as there are learners in your group, so that everyone gets a chance to perform the solo section.

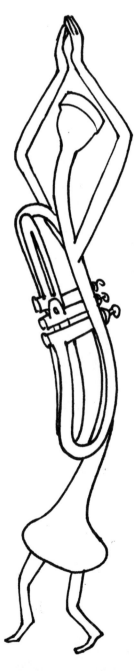

Bhangra Beat

Play with a light swing to create Bhangra feel ♩ = 144

K Charlton

Group A
Jalapeño Salsa

Salsa literally means 'sauce', and the term encompasses many different Latin rhythms and styles. Salsa began in Cuba and was influenced by African and Spanish music, as well as the dance music of neighbouring Dominica and Colombia. In the 1970s, musicians in New York combined traditional salsa with rock and funk music to create the salsa music we recognise today. The classic salsa band is made up of vocals, piano, bass, brass section, and percussion.

When you play this piece, don't rush the rhythm, but stay on top of the beat, playing against the syncopation in the bass line. Make sure you hold the last notes of bars 5, 9, 11 and 13 for their full value. You should play the repeated section as many times as there are learners in your group, so that everyone gets a chance to perform the solo section.

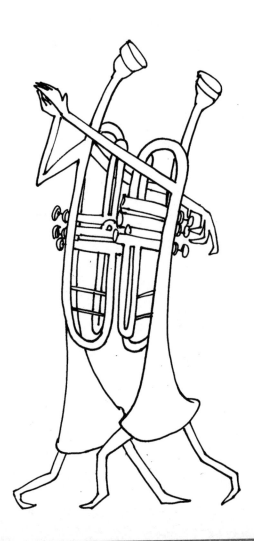

Jalapeño Salsa

♩ = 120

O Weston

Tutti

mf

La - tin beats_ cre - ate the sal - sa mu - sic groove!

Solo

f

First it swings_ and then it gent - ly sways,_ the rhy - thm

swings and sways_ to make the sal - sa mu - sic groove!

f

Next a loud phrase, *p* then a quiet phrase.

Repeat as necessary

f

Next a loud phrase, *p* then a quiet phrase.

Tutti (last time only)

f

First it swings_ and then it gent - ly sways, the rhy - thm

swings and sways_ to make the sal - sa mu - sic groove!

Group A
Wedding March

There are brass bands all over India who play for weddings and other celebrations, performing songs from Bollywood films. Every large town or city in India has its 'band shops' - the place you go to book a band for your son's wedding. The band accompanies the groom and his family on a colourful procession or *baraat* to meet the bride for the ceremony. The bigger the band, the more the family can show off!

Wedding March is in a minor key (typical in Bollywood music), and you should play the opening section in a brisk, marching band style. Play the melody in the solo section *legato*, making sure that the long notes are full length, breathing after the tied note in bar 11 if you need to. In the ending section from bar 25, play the riffs in a heavy, accented way, like a big brass section. You should play the repeated section as many times as there are learners in your group, so that everyone gets a chance to perform the solo section.

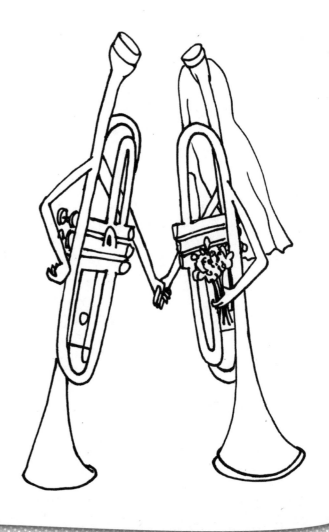

Wedding March

Play like an Indian wedding brass band ♩ = 150

K Charlton

Group B - Technical Piece Timekeeper

The pieces in Group B are Technical Pieces. These have a different structure to Group A pieces, and a specific technical element has been identified for each one. It is important that you demonstrate this to the examiner when you perform your Technical Piece.

Technical Pieces are divided into four phrases, marked 1, 2, 3 and 4 on the score. In the exam, the examiner allocates a different phrase to each member of your group. You then perform the Technical Piece with each of you playing your allocated phrase. The phrases are not allocated in advance, so it is important that you learn the whole piece.

If there are two or three members in your group, the examiner allocates only the first two or three phrases and then stops the backing track after each of you has played. If there are four members, the examiner allocates all four phrases, and the group should also play the final *tutti* phrase together. The *tutti* phrase is not assessed, so don't worry if you don't get a chance to play it.

Technical element you will be assessed on in Timekeeper: sustaining longer phrases

Phrases are the 'sentences' that up make music. This piece requires you to observe the phrases and, where possible, avoid breaking them up. This means that you should try not to breathe until you get to the end of each phrase. All of the phrases in this piece are four bars long, but it would be fine to take a breath after two bars. For example, you could breathe at the end of bar 6 in the phrase that runs from bar 5 to bar 8 - think of this four-bar 'sentence' as having a comma after two bars. Try not to take big, noisy gasps - see if you can take your breath quietly so as not to disturb the longer phrase.

Timekeeper

Pop ballad ♩ = 110

O Weston

1

Keep in time. Don't you step out____ of line.____

Keep in time____ now____ Ooo yeah.

2

Tune feels real slow, give it the space____ to grow.____

Don't rush the rhy - thm, no____ Ooo yeah.

3

Keep in time. Don't you step out____ of line.____

Keep in time____ now____ Ooo yeah.

29 **4**

Tune   feels   real   slow,___   give   it   the   space___   to   grow.__

33

Don't   rush   the   rhy - thm,   no____   Ooo   yeah.

37 Tutti

Don't   rush   the   rhy - thm,   no____   keep   the   ti - ming   slow.____

Group B - Technical Piece Articulation Holiday

The pieces in Group B are Technical Pieces. These have a different structure to Group A pieces, and a specific technical element has been identified for each one. It is important that you demonstrate this to the examiner when you perform your Technical Piece.

Technical Pieces are divided into four phrases, marked 1, 2, 3 and 4 on the score. In the exam, the examiner allocates a different phrase to each member of your group. You then perform the Technical Piece with each of you playing your allocated phrase. The phrases are not allocated in advance, so it is important that you learn the whole piece.

If there are two or three members in your group, the examiner allocates only the first two or three phrases and then stops the backing track after each of you has played. If there are four members, the examiner allocates all four phrases, and the group should also play the final *tutti* phrase together. The *tutti* phrase is not assessed, so don't worry if you don't get a chance to play it.

Technical element you will be assessed on in Articulation Holiday: articulation

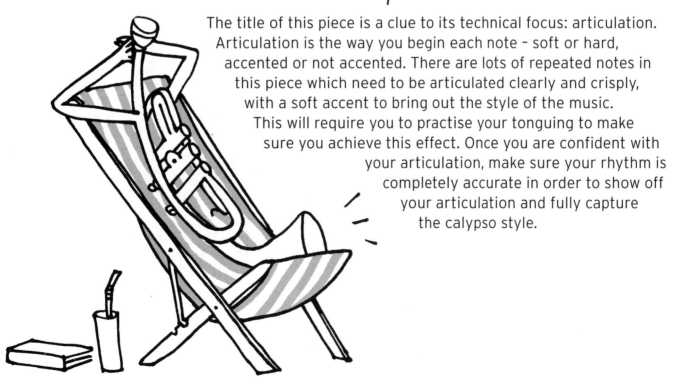

The title of this piece is a clue to its technical focus: articulation. Articulation is the way you begin each note - soft or hard, accented or not accented. There are lots of repeated notes in this piece which need to be articulated clearly and crisply, with a soft accent to bring out the style of the music. This will require you to practise your tonguing to make sure you achieve this effect. Once you are confident with your articulation, make sure your rhythm is completely accurate in order to show off your articulation and fully capture the calypso style.

Articulation Holiday

Calypso ♩ = 116

R Forsyth and M Simpson

29 **4**

Listen to___ re - lax - ing tunes,_ play a - long___ and feel the groove,

33

what a per - fect ho - li - day,___ Ca - rib - be - an cruise yeh!

37 Tutti

f

it's a___ per - fect ho - li - day;___ Ca - rib - be - an cruise, yeah!

The Musicianship Skills tests

Copyback

Your group must choose between **Copyback** and **Improvising** for the Musicianship Skills test. (Please note that the whole group must choose the same test.) **Copyback** involves taking it in turns to play along with a backing track, repeating four short musical phrases straight after you have heard each one. You will not have seen or heard the phrases before, but you will be familiar with the backing track - it will be taken from a piece in this book, or one very similar in style or genre.

In the exam, the examiner gives each member of your group a notated version of the phrases, and the group as a whole is given 30 seconds to study or try out the phrases. The examiner also gives the order in which the members of your group should perform the test. The group then performs the test twice: first time for practice and second time for assessment. The backing track runs throughout the test, and the examiner will start and stop it for both performances.

Opposite are some example tests. You can find backing tracks for the example tests on the CD in this book.

Note for teachers

The Copyback example tests have been provided as a guide to what the test will be like in the exam. Please note that the test in the exam will be different to these examples, with a different backing track.

You are advised to use the example tests with your learners to help familiarise them with the format of the test. Each example test contains material for four different candidates, so try assigning a different performance order to your learners each time you use the example tests.

Copyback - Example 1

Track 16

Candidate 1

Listen 1st time, play 2nd time.

Candidate 2

Listen 1st time, play 2nd time.

Candidate 3

Listen 1st time, play 2nd time.

Candidate 4

Listen 1st time, play 2nd time.

Copyback – Example 2

The Musicianship Skills Tests

Improvising

The **Improvising** test involves taking it in turns to improvise over a backing track taken from a piece in this book, or one very similar in style or genre.

In the exam, the examiner gives each member of your group a chord chart and plays a few bars of the backing track to give you a sense of the tempo and feel. The group as a whole is then given 30 seconds to prepare and try out some ideas. Three pitches are suggested on the chord chart for you to use in your improvisation – you can choose to use these pitches, these and others, or a completely different set of pitches. You are free to discuss your choices with each other in the 30 seconds' preparation time, and your choices won't affect the marks you are given – you are marked purely on the quality of your improvisation, whichever notes you use.

The examiner gives the order in which the members of your group should perform the test. You then perform the test twice: first time for practice and second time for assessment. The examiner starts and stops the backing track for both performances, and also indicates when each of you should start and stop improvising. As a guide, each of you should improvise for about 16 bars.

Over the page are some example tests. You can find backing tracks for the example tests on the CD in this book.

Note for teachers

The backing tracks for the Improvising test are long loops of music, usually a repeating eight-bar chord sequence. To help learners know where they are in the music and structure their improvisations accordingly, the examiner will direct each learner to start improvising at the beginning of the chord sequence. This should be your guide when preparing learners for the Improvising test.

The backing tracks can also be used as a resource for different kinds of improvising, so try giving your learners different sets of pitches for them to experiment with. How do different stimuli affect their improvisations? You could also try developing their improvising skills by giving them rhythms instead of pitches, or even visual images.

Improvising – Example 1

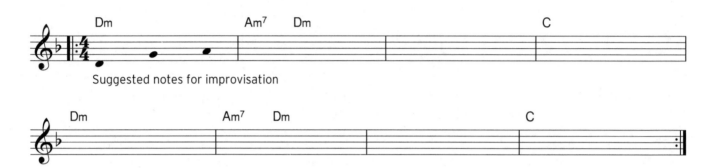

Suggested notes for improvisation

Improvising – Example 2

Track
19

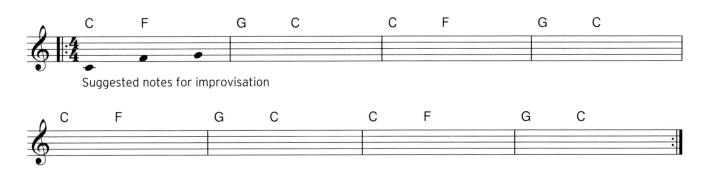

Suggested notes for improvisation

CD track listing

1 Tuning note (B♭)
2 **Township Time** (backing track - 2 candidates)
3 **Township Time** (backing track - 3 candidates)
4 **Township Time** (backing track - 4 candidates)
5 **Bhangra Beat** (backing track - 2 candidates)
6 **Bhangra Beat** (backing track - 3 candidates)
7 **Bhangra Beat** (backing track - 4 candidates)
8 **Jalapeño Salsa** (backing track - 2 candidates)
9 **Jalapeño Salsa** (backing track - 3 candidates)
10 **Jalapeño Salsa** (backing track - 4 candidates)
11 **Wedding March** (backing track - 2 candidates)
12 **Wedding March** (backing track - 3 candidates)
13 **Wedding March** (backing track - 4 candidates)
14 **Timekeeper** (backing track)
15 **Articulation Holiday** (backing track)
16 Copyback - example 1 (backing track)
17 Copyback - example 2 (backing track)
18 Improvising - example 1 (backing track)
19 Improvising - example 2 (backing track)

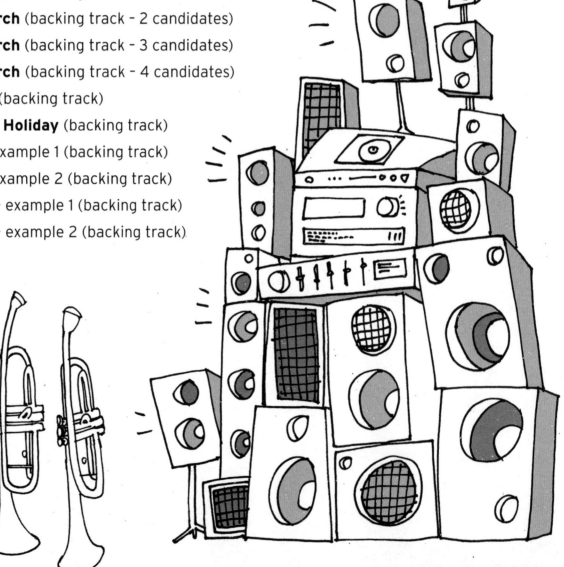